To Taylor,

May you always
have a friend.

Eva Schmidler

PRAISE FOR THE BOOK

"Eva Schmidler has fashioned a charming tale that will appeal to younger readers and their parents. I can envision a mother reading it to her child or a teacher to her class and I'm sure the story would generate lively discussions."

Bob Singer, former head of design, Hanna-Barbera Prods.

"I thought it was a wonderful story with a great moral message. Children of all ages will enjoy this heartwarming story of friendship."

Nicole Burk, Second Grade Teacher, Laurel Hill Primary, Mt. Pleasant, SC

"Imaginative, touching, full of understanding and acceptance. A refreshing story of an unlikely friendship leading to discovery and adventure. Children and adults alike can learn some valuable lessons from this story. Tiny is destined to become a classic."

Tony Seaman, Director, University Publishing Center (retired). The University of Mississippi. Oxford, MS

"This was the best book I have ever read. I love this book. You will love this book so much you won't put it down. This book is the most interesting, awesome book. I recommend every kid who loves animals read this book."

Marissa Corcoran, age 9, 4th grade, St. Anne Catholic School in Tomball, TX

"I liked this book, because it showed how different people and different animals can have so much in common. It would be a fun book for children six and older."

Sara Cramer, age 9, 4th grade, St. George Episcopal School, Milner, GA

SPECIAL FEATURE

Tiny Makes a Friend contains subjects that are common to all children. At the end of the book is a section called *ASK YOURSELF* designed to help readers focus on these aspects of learning and life.

Tiny Makes
a Friend

Tiny Makes a Friend

EVA SCHMIDLER

This is a work of fiction. All of the characters, names, incidents,
organizations, and dialogue in this novel are either the products
of the author's imagination or are used fictitiously.

Archway Publishing books may be ordered through booksellers or by contacting:

Archway Publishing
1663 Liberty Drive
Bloomington, IN 47403
www.archwaypublishing.com
1 (888) 242-5904

Illustrations by Toby Mikle.

ISBN: 978-1-4808-3058-5 (sc)
ISBN: 978-1-4808-3059-2 (e)

Library of Congress Control Number: 2016908718

Print information available on the last page.

Archway Publishing rev. date: 8/30/2016

To
RICHARD AND KATE
WITH LOVE

CONTENTS

1

BREAKING THE RULE

NOT TOO LONG AGO, THERE WAS A MOUSE family that lived in an animal refuge park. The refuge park was at the edge of a friendly forest where many animals lived and played. The mouse family made their modest home in the wall of a cage where a tiger lived. Mr. and Mrs. Mouse had seven

children who were always hungry. There just never seemed to be enough food to fill so many tummies. Every day, Papa Mouse would say to Mama Mouse, "I must go out and look for something to feed my big family," and that

is what he did. But try as he may, day after day, he would come home with very little food for such a large family.

On the side of the wall where the tiger lived were several cages separated so other animals could have their own place to live. The mouse hole opened into the cage of Mr. Tiger—that's what the mouse children called him. Through their hole, they could see that the tiger was well taken care of by keepers who loved animals. The keepers enjoyed taking care of Mr. Tiger because they knew there weren't many tigers left in the world, and each was important. They also took good care of the lion cubs, the young leopard, and the monkeys in the cages next to Mr. Tiger's. These animals and many others that lived in the refuge park didn't have any mothers or fathers or were old or not wanted. Every day, the mouse children would watch a

nice keeper bring Mr. Tiger lots of good food to eat, and Mr. Tiger would eat every bit of it.

Each day in the mouse house, Mama Mouse would put what little there was to eat on the table and call to her children, "It's time to eat. Don't forget to wash your hands."

All the children would then scurry about trying to be first at the table, and every time, the youngest mouse would be the last to sit down. This youngest mouse was so small that his two sisters and four brothers all called him Tiny. At first he really didn't like to be called Tiny, because his real name was Tim, but after a while he got used to it and thought

it made him special.

When the children were all seated around the table, Mama Mouse would say, "Children, remember to eat slowly and take only your portion so everyone will have something to eat."

But each time, Tiny's

older brothers and sisters were quick to eat all of the meager meal. *All I ever get to eat are the crumbs!* thought Tiny.

Tiny could *never* get enough to eat, and he was *always* hungry. After lunch, Tiny's brothers and sisters would run off to play, but Tiny never joined them. "I wish I could run and play like my brothers and sisters, but my tummy aches and I'm just too hungry. I don't have any energy to play. All I can think about is *food*," said Tiny to himself. Tiny would then go to his favorite place by the mouse hole to sit and look out into Mr. Tiger's cage, where he could see all the food Mr. Tiger had to eat.

Seeing Mr. Tiger's food made Tiny even hungrier. His brothers and sisters often teased him and mockingly said, "Look at Tiny! He has his eye on the tiger's food, but he's a scaredy cat and too chicken to go get some." Then to be mean, they added, "We dare you to go into Mr. Tiger's house and nip some of his delicious-looking food."

Mamas and papas always seem to know what is in their children's heads, and Tiny's mama and papa were no different. Mama Mouse told Tiny, "Don't you *ever* go into Mr. Tiger's cage. He is very big and you are very little, and it would be very dangerous."

Papa agreed and said, "He could swish his tail and knock you across the room, or he might accidentally step on you with his great paw and squash you. It just isn't safe for you to go into his cage. We love you all dearly and don't want any of you ever to get hurt."

Day after day, Tiny would watch from his mouse hole as the keepers would bring Mr. Tiger's food. He would see a big bone with meat on it and all kinds of delicious-looking foods. Tiny would think to himself, *Oh, how I wish I could taste those round red things, and the yellow and green things, and oh, so many things I have never seen.* Day after day, Tiny's eyes would get big, and his mouth would water as he watched the tiger eat and eat and eat until he was full. *I must figure out a way so I can have just one little taste of Mr. Tiger's food,* thought Tiny. *I'll show my brothers and sisters just who is afraid to go into Mr. Tiger's cage.*

One day Tiny was talking to his mother and

said, "Oh, Mama, why can't I sneak into Mr. Tiger's cage and take just a little bite of his food? I could go very quietly when he is taking a nap. He couldn't hurt me if he is asleep. He has so much to eat. He will never miss it."

Mama knew how Tiny longed to eat like the tiger next door, but she also knew the danger, so she looked at little Tiny and said, "Timmy"—that's what his mother called him—"it would be just *too* danger-ous. You are very little now, but you are growing and soon you will be big enough to find your own food." Day after day, Tiny watched Mr. Tiger eat his lunch and thought about what his mother had said.

It wasn't long before Tiny was so very, very hungry, and his tummy was making all kinds of noises. He just couldn't stand it any longer. He said to himself, "I made up my mind. I might be little and it might be dangerous, but I am *really* hungry. It just isn't fair for Mr. Tiger to have so much to eat when I have so little. Tomorrow, I'll take my chances and just venture into Mr. Tiger's cage and have a bite of his food. I don't care if he is awake or not!"

The next day, Tiny was watching from his doorway as Mr. Tiger's keeper brought him his lunch. Tiny saw the food, and his eyes got big and bigger. His great hunger made him *very* brave. In a flash, Tiny scurried out through the hole of his house to where Mr. Tiger was eating and began to eat beside him.

He tasted the red apples, the yellow squash, the green beans, the meat, and all of the delicious food he had been watching Mr. Tiger eat for so long. *Oh, how delicious it all tastes. Mr. Tiger is so lucky to have so much food*, thought Tiny. *I could just eat and eat and eat.* And that is what he did.

Mr. Tiger looked up and couldn't believe his eyes. Imagine, a tiny mouse eating *his* food!

At first, Mr. Tiger just looked at Tiny with amazement, but then he got closer and carefully sniffed him. Tiny didn't even notice. He was too busy eating and chomping away. Then Mr. Tiger gave Tiny a nudge to see if he would go away. Tiny didn't budge, and he didn't stop eating. Mr. Tiger didn't know what to do. Tiny was not afraid and paid no attention to anything Mr. Tiger did to make him go away. This was Tiny's first big meal *ever*, and he wasn't going to be interrupted. He kept eating and eating and chomping and chomping.

Now Mr. Tiger had a problem. He was hungry too and wanted to eat his lunch. *How am I going to eat with this little fellow in the way? Nothing I do makes him go away.* Finally, Mr. Tiger thought to himself,

This little mouse must be really *hungry to come into my cage. He is so tiny, he really can't eat much. I'll just leave him alone and eat along beside him. Besides, I've never had company for lunch before.* So there

they sat together, the big tiger and the tiny mouse sharing a meal.

When Tiny had his fill and his tummy was so full he had to burp, he looked up into Mr. Tiger's eyes and said, "Thank you."

Mr. Tiger was curious and asked, "Why aren't you afraid of me? Why did you come into my cage and eat on my lunch?

Tiny introduced himself, as polite children do, and told Mr. Tiger the story of how his father searched for food every day and how little his family had to eat. Mr. Tiger listened and thought about his early  days when he was hungry before he was brought to live at the refuge park. He would never want any other animal to be as hungry as he had been. When Mr. Tiger spoke, he said in a kind and gentle voice, "Tiny, I will be happy to share my lunch with you and your family. You may visit me anytime."

"Thank you, Mr. Tiger. You are very kind," said Tiny as he disappeared through the mouse hole and home again.

Tiny was very careful not to say anything to his brothers and sisters because he knew he had disobeyed his mother and they would tell on him.

That night, after his brothers and sisters finished their dinner, they wondered why Tiny didn't rush for the crumbs. Later, at bedtime, after the lights were out, they gathered around Tiny and asked, "Why didn't you eat? You are always so hungry."

Tiny took a deep breath, stood up straight, and looking right at his brothers and sisters, said, "Today I just made up my mind to take a chance and go into Mr. Tiger's cage. He has so much to eat, I thought he wouldn't notice if I took a few bites of his lunch." As Tiny told his story, his brothers' and sisters' eyes got bigger and bigger until they were as round as little balls of cheese.

When Tiny finished his story, the only thing they could say was, "*Wow*!" and let out a big cheer. "We *never* thought you would actually take our dare and really go into Mr. Tiger's cage. What a surprise! You are *so very* brave! We could *never* be as brave as you!"

From that night on, Tiny's brothers and sisters had a great respect for him and never, *ever* teased him again. They were so proud of their little brother. Long into the night, Tiny's brothers and sisters thought about his story of meeting Mr. Tiger and how very nice he was to share his lunch. Finally, they all fell asleep and dreamed of one day meeting Mr. Tiger.

2

A FRIENDSHIP IS MADE

TINY MOUSE WAS VERY EXCITED ABOUT meeting Mr. Tiger and being invited back to share his lunch. Still, if he wanted to visit again and bring his brothers and sisters, he would first have to confess to his mother that he had disobeyed her. The next day, Tiny slowly crawled to his mother and in a trembling and shaky voice said, "Mommy, I have something to tell you."

Mommy bent down and took Timmy in her arms, "Don't be afraid, Timmy. You know you can tell me anything. Now, tell me, what's the matter?"

She then listened carefully as Tiny confessed what he had done. He quickly added, "Mr. Tiger is really very nice and invited all of us to visit and share his lunch. He said he is lonely and had never

14

met a mouse before. Please, Mama, can I go and visit him again?"

Mother just looked at her little boy with amazement and with an understanding smile said, "Timmy, you disobeyed, but I know how hungry you were, so I can't be angry with you. I am just thankful you were not hurt and pleased that Mr. Tiger  is so nice. Yes, you may visit Mr. Tiger whenever you want ... and it was very nice of him to invite your family to share his food."

After that, Tiny began to visit Mr. Tiger regularly. They became best friends and felt very comfortable being together. Imagine that! A tiny mouse and a big tiger being best friends!

One morning Mama Mouse said to Papa, "I think it is time we take our family to meet Mr. Tiger. Tiny has been so happy since they met and says that Mr. Tiger wants to meet us."

Papa frowned and said, "Mama, I don't think it's a

good idea to get too friendly with a tiger. It's just too dangerous for us little folks. Tigers are so *big*!"

Mama reminded him that Tiny had been visiting Mr. Tiger and no harm had come to him. Papa thought about it for a few minutes and had to agree with Mama that maybe they should all meet Mr. Tiger. Papa said, "Okay, let's go meet Mr. Tiger."

Mama called her children together and told them the news. After the keeper brought Mr. Tiger's lunch, they dressed in their finest, left their mouse hole, and entered Mr. Tiger's cage. Mr. Tiger watched the mouse family come in and thought, *Wow! I've never had so much company at one time.*

As the mouse children got closer to the tiger, they all thought, *Wow! He's so* big*!*

Mama and Papa were very polite as they introduced their family. "We'd like you to meet our sons, Mark, Matt, Mitch, and Mike, and our daughters, Sue and Sally. Of course you know our youngest, Tim."

As each child was introduced, Mr. Tiger nodded and held the tip of his tail in an upright position and slowly let it sway back and forth. This was Mr. Tiger's way of saying, "Welcome, I want to be your friend." He then invited his new family of friends to share his lunch. The children were so excited they just scurried from one item to another, sniffing, nibbling, and tasting. Mama tried, but couldn't make them mind

their manners. Once the children satisfied their tummies, they began looking at Mr. Tiger.

Seeing the curious look in their eyes, he said, "It's okay. You can climb on me to get a closer look. I don't mind."

They thought this was great and were not shy at all. First, they climbed on his claws. Each child had his own claw to stand on as he examined the long, sharp nail. They quickly realized Mr. Tiger's paws were not something to play with. Then they ran around to examine his tail. The children made a game of trying to see who could guess the number of rings on it. Later, Mr. Tiger lay down so they could climb on his back and up to his head. Mark crawled into one of the big ears, stood up, and shouted, "Look at me! His ear is so big I can stand up."

This tickled Mr. Tiger, causing his head to shake really fast. In their fright, the children quickly grabbed a handful of fur and hung on with all of their might. Once the shaking stopped, they all laughed and laughed. When it was time to go, Mama, Papa, and each of their children politely thanked Mr. Tiger and promised to return. Then, waving good-bye, they disappeared into their hole.

When Tiny's brothers and sisters were not busy playing or helping their mother, they would go with him to visit Mr. Tiger and share his lunch. The mouse children really enjoyed tasting the different foods the keeper brought. Each time, there seemed to be something new they had never tasted before. Mr. Tiger was always happy to have company and enjoyed listening to his mouse friends talk about the games they played and the fun they had together.

One afternoon, after lunch, when they were just sitting around, Mr. Tiger began to talk. He began to tell them about how he came to live in the rescue center. "I don't remember everything, because I was very young, but I do remember living in the jungle with my mom and dad and lots of aunts and uncles and some cousins. My cousins were older and didn't want to play with me, so I was often lonesome." Mr. Tiger continued, "One day my parents led me deep

into the jungle where the trees were tall and the brush was thick. I could hardly see the daylight. It was scary. My parents said they wanted to hide me from men who were looking for tigers to take away in big cages. They found a place for me behind some bushes where they thought I would be safe."

"They told me to lay very quiet and stay hidden, saying, 'We'll come back for you when the men are gone.' Then they gave me a big hug and a gentle lick and left. Frightened and not knowing what would happen, I did as I was told. Soon it was very dark, and I heard sounds of the night. Birds called to each other, small animals awakened, and leaves rustled. I was scared. I tried to stay awake, but I dozed off to sleep. A loud cry woke me. It sounded like my mom and dad. I didn't know what to do. I wanted to run, but I was afraid. Then I heard excited voices, which must have been those of the hunters. Frightened and exhausted, I did just what my mommy and daddy said and lay very still. Soon I fell asleep. In the morning when I awoke, I looked around and waited for my mom and dad to come get me, but they didn't come. I was hungry, afraid, and all alone. I walked around hoping to see my aunts and uncles or even my cousins, but they were nowhere to be found. I tried to find food for myself, but I was young and didn't know how to hunt. Every day I became weaker and weaker until I could no longer move."

Tiny and his brothers and sisters listened with tears in their eyes.

They just couldn't imagine being all alone in a big jungle without a mother and father and not being able to find food or have anyone to help or talk to. They were always so warm and comfortable in their home in the walls of Mr. Tiger's cage. Each brother and sister was very still and quiet as Mr. Tiger continued.

"I was so weak from not having anything to eat.

I lay crying and began thinking that I would never see my mom and dad again and would soon die of hunger when some people heard my cry and found me. They gently picked me up, stroked my back, and gave me milk to drink. Then they put me in a warm, comfortable cage in the back of a big truck.

I had no idea what would happen next and was too weak to be afraid. I was just thankful to have something to eat. We drove for a long time until we came to this rescue park, where I have lived ever since. The keeper who first took care of me named me Toby, and I used to sit on her lap while she petted and played with me. When I got bigger, though, she stopped coming. Now a keeper just brings my food and never has time to play. I was very lonely until you came."

Mark, Matt, Mitch, Mike, Tiny, and their sisters, Sue and Sally, felt so sorry for their friend growing up in a cage without parents or aunts and uncles to teach him the ways of a tiger. He was big, all right, but not at all aggressive and frightening, as their mother had warned them he would be. Toby was shy and friendly.

Tiny spoke for his brothers and sisters. "Mr. Tiger, we will be your friends and play with you."

"Oh, thank you! Please call me Toby. Would you all like to take a ride on my back?"

With that, the mice ran up Toby's tail and onto his back. Not wanting to harm his little friends, Toby began to walk slowly around his cage. The mice shouted, "Faster, faster!" Oh, how they jiggled and giggled as Toby ran faster and faster.

Finally, when Toby was dizzy and the brothers and sisters could no longer hold on, Toby stopped. Mark, Matt, Mitch, Mike, Tiny, and sisters Sue and Sally slid down Toby's tail, landing in a heap as the room swirled and whirled around and around in their heads. Soon they heard their mom call, "It's time to come home. Tell Mr. Tiger good night." And that is what they did.

3

A BOLD ADVENTURE

TINY MOUSE AND TOBY TIGER HAD BEEN best friends for a long time and were no longer little. Tiny's older brothers had already left home. Nobody knew exactly how old Toby was, but he was growing up too. The two friends often talked and wondered about what the world was like beyond the cage where they lived. Each day they were becoming more restless and more curious to find out.

Tiny's birthday was coming soon, and he was so excited. "Imagine me, Tiny, a teenager!"

He could hardly wait to tell Toby and to start making birthday plans. Tiny rushed into Toby's house, but Toby wasn't there. Toby was *always* home. The only time Toby's door was opened was when the keeper brought food. Today, however, the door was open, and Toby was gone. Tiny's heart skipped a beat. He didn't want to lose his best friend.

Not knowing what to do, Tiny scurried all around the cage, sniffing for some sign of his friend. "Where could he be? Will he come back? Why didn't he say good-bye? I'll just sit right down by the bars so I can see out and wait and hope for his return."

Soon Tiny saw two keepers walking by and talking. Luckily, they stopped close to Toby's cage. He could hear them saying, "How do you like this new kid we have working with us?"

The other one answered, "I don't know. He's young

and doesn't have any experience working with the big cats. One good thing, though, he doesn't mind taking them out for exercise. He puts a chain around their neck and takes them walking around the reserve. Sometimes he pulls hard on the chain and pokes the cats with his stick if they don't go where he wants them to."

"Yeah, exercise is good for the animals, but not if you pull and poke them. I'm afraid a cat will get angry and attack him one of these days. He needs to learn to be more patient."

"You are so right, and when he brings their food, he just shoves it in the cage and slams the door."

Tiny could hardly believe his ears. At least he knew where Toby was and that he would return, but he didn't like the thought of Toby not being treated very nicely. "Toby is such a good and gentle friend. He shouldn't be treated that way. He isn't fierce like other tigers and shouldn't be pulled around and poked with a stick."

Before long, the new keeper brought Toby back, and Tiny saw how he just opened the door and pushed him in. When the keeper closed the door and left, Tiny ran to Toby and snuggled up close as he blurted out, "I was so worried that I would never see you again. I'm so glad you're back." Toby lowered his head and gently licked Tiny, letting him know how much he appreciated his little friend. "While I was waiting, I heard two keepers talking about the new one. They said he likes to take the big cats for a walk but doesn't treat them very nicely. I saw how he just pushed you through the door with his stick. Did he hurt you?"

Toby looked very sad as he said, "Ralph, my new

keeper, has been coming only a few days. He is not at all like the keepers who found and raised me. I don't like it here anymore."

Tiny snuggled closer to Toby. It was the only way he knew to comfort his big friend. Toby was relieved to have someone he could talk to and who seemed to understand.

When Tiny went home, he told his mother about Ralph. She gently put her arm around him, saying, "Timmy, Toby needs you now. He is going through a difficult time and needs to talk to someone he can trust. As his friend, you will be able to help him. I'm sure that you will think of some way to make Toby feel better."

That night, Tiny had a hard time falling asleep. He was busy thinking of a way to help his friend Toby.

Tiny remembered that before he met Toby, his mother said tigers were big and strong and could do what they wanted. This was hard to believe, because Toby never showed his power. He didn't have to. He was always treated nicely, was happy, and liked his home. He never made trouble for his keepers, but now maybe it was time he acted more like other tigers. Tiny had a plan.

In the morning, Tiny paid Toby a visit. Toby looked sad and not his cheerful self. "Cheer up, Toby. I have an idea. My birthday is coming soon, and I want to do something *really* special. I have never been anywhere except my house and your house. I think it is time we have a look around to see what's outside of this reserve. On your walks with Ralph, did you notice where the gates are? Why don't we just go out exploring and have ourselves a real adventure?"

"Oh, my," said Toby. "Wouldn't we get in trouble?"

"Come on, Toby, you're big and strong and can do anything you want."

"I'm not so sure. I'll have to think about this," said Toby.

That afternoon when Toby was on his walk with Ralph, he thought about Tiny's idea. He pulled away so he could walk nearer the fence. Ralph didn't like this, but Toby didn't care; he knew he was more powerful. He looked very carefully to see where the gates were and if they could be easily opened. He was alert and noticed every-thing. He noticed the keepers walking around the yard and where they lived. He even took a glance beyond the fence and wondered what it would be like to run free and explore the jungle. By the time Toby returned home, he had made up his mind. *Yes, I will go exploring with Tiny*, he thought to himself.

The next day, when Tiny returned, Toby told him,

"You're right, Tiny. We've talked about exploring, and your birthday is a perfect time to start. This will be my birthday present to you."

"Oh, *thank you*, Toby! You just made me *very* happy. This birthday will really be special. It will be the best ever!"

"Now all we have to do is plan very carefully. We don't want anything to go wrong, and we sure don't want to get caught."

After some serious thinking, they decided to go on the night of Tiny's birthday after everyone had gone to sleep. Tiny said, "When you are on your walk with Ralph, I'll place a bone in your doorway to keep the door from closing tight. Ralph is so careless, he won't even notice. Toby, with your strong paws, you will be able to pull the door open for our escape. We have only one more challenge before the plan is complete. How can we get beyond the fence that surrounds this reserve?"

Toby wagged his tail quickly from side to side to show his excitement. "I know how. On my walk, I saw a section of the fence that was worn and needed fixing. It is way off in a corner by some bushes and not very noticeable. I'm sure that, with a push from me, it will break and we can go out."

"Hooray!" shouted Tiny. "Our plan is complete! Now all we have to do is wait until my birthday."

At first the days seemed long and it felt as if the big date would never come, but the time did pass, and it was finally Tiny's birthday. That evening, after Tiny's family had finished eating the special birthday

dinner that his mom had prepared, the family gathered around Tiny and sang, "Happy Birthday" and gave him presents. Tiny opened his presents and thanked his brothers and sisters. It was late when they finished play-  ing with his new games, and it was time for bed. Tiny gave everyone a big hug, thanked them again, and said good night.

Tiny lay in bed and waited until the house was quiet and everyone was sound asleep. Then he slipped through the mouse hole and into Toby's cage. Toby was ready and waiting. They glanced at each other as their hearts beat a little faster. Without saying a word, the best friends got right to work on their plan. With Tiny holding on to the hairs of his broad shoulders, Toby pawed at the heavy door until it opened wide enough for them to squeeze through.

Once they were out in the yard, Toby headed straight for the bushes in the corner and the worn fence. Being careful not to damage the bushes, he easily pushed through the fence. When Toby and Tiny were safely on the other side of the fence, they looked at each other and let out a *big* breath. "*Phew!*"

You see, all this time, they had hardly taken a breath for fear of being caught. Realizing they were now free to roam about, they wagged their tails and grinned with delight as they started on their adventure.

Slowly, they began to wander through the jungle. Their path was lit only by the shine of the moon coming through the leaves of the tall trees. Toby's stiff whiskers parted the brush as he moved through the forest. They smelled the cool, fresh air and felt the dewy moisture on their fur. They heard the crunch of twigs and leaves beneath Toby's short, muscled legs. His long, slender body glided effort-lessly through the thick brush. Toby began to stop often as he heard strange and yet somehow familiar sounds of the night in the jungle. Toby and Tiny did not say a word as they continued moving through the jungle. They were too busy listening and feeling the excitement of being alone in the darkness with all the strange smells and sounds. Grasshoppers chirped and pattered as they passed. In the distance they heard the trumpet of an elephant's call. In the trees, they heard monkeys chattering loudly to one another. They heard parrots talking and owls hooting.

After a while, they heard the hiss of a snake as he slithered through the brush near the edge of a river. Toby and Tiny were glad to find water because their throats were dry with fear. The  water was cool and tasted sweet. Toby was enjoying his drink when Tiny saw ripples in the water and something moving slowly toward them.

He pulled on Toby's hairs and whispered, "Something big is in the water, and it's coming this way! Let's go!"

As the crocodile glided near the bank, the frogs croaked loudly and the flies buzzed about from their resting place. Toby looked up, saw the long, dark movement in the water, and agreed that it *was* time to go. As they hurried back to the reserve, they heard birds singing to one another, apes gibbering, and the hyenas laughing.

It wasn't long before Tiny and Toby were through the fence and back in Toby's cage, safe and sound. "Boy! Was *that* fun! This is one birthday I'll *never* forget!" Toby agreed by giving Tiny a gentle and loving nudge. The friends were so filled with excitement they chatted long into the night about their adventure.

It was early morning when Tiny decided he'd better scurry home before his family missed him. Before Tiny left, the friends agreed to explore again, hoping that one day they would meet one of Toby's cousins.

4

BITTERSWEET GOOD-BYES

TINY AND TOBY HAD NO IDEA HOW THEIR walk in the jungle would change the way they felt about living in a cage. They had experienced freedom and wanted more. A few weeks later when they went for another walk, they discovered the broken fence had been repaired. "Drats!" The only freedom Toby had now was his walks with Ralph. As Ralph got more experience and less afraid of the big cats, he learned to guide the animals gently with his stick and not poke them. Toby was happy again and now looked forward to his walks. Everything seemed to be just right. Even Tiny began exploring the grounds. Being little, he could go almost anywhere without being seen. He really enjoyed his newfound freedom.

One day when Tiny came to visit, Toby said, "Ralph didn't come today. I miss my walk."

"I'll go to the keepers' cabin to see what I can find out," volunteered Tiny as he scurried off through the bars of the cage and across the yard.

Before long, he returned with the news that Ralph had left the reserve. He heard the keepers say, "He was just here for the summer and never really planned to stay." The keepers talked about how much Ralph learned from the animals and that he might get a job with a circus.

Not long after Ralph left, special keepers began to

take an interest in Toby. Tiny learned that their job was to take Toby beyond the reserve and into the jungle. This news excited Toby because he knew that was where he belonged. Whenever they came to visit, he made sure he was on his best behavior. One day, they took Toby out of his cage, walked him to a big truck,

and guided him into another cage. *Uh, oh*, thought Toby. *This is it. This is the day I will be set free.*

Toby lay quietly in the cage as they drove down the road and to the jungle. They couldn't go deep into the jungle with the truck, but they were able to go a little way. When the truck stopped, Toby was led out of the cage. He waited while they put the cage in the jungle and led him back into it. Then they left. Toby wondered, "What is going on? Why are they leaving me caged in the jungle?" Toby soon found out. He was simply sitting in his cage when two curious tigers came up to him. They slowly walked around his cage, sniffing as they went. The tigers carefully looked him over and then wagged their tails in greeting. Toby responded with a wag of his tail and a soft chuff in response to let them know that he, too, was pleased to see them. It had been so long since he was with other tigers.

All the while, Toby was just as curious. "Could this be real? Could they be my cousins?" The cats stayed until their curiosity was satisfied, then turned and disappeared into the jungle. Toby felt more alone now than he had ever felt. "Why are they treating me this way? Why can't they just set me free so I can go off with these tigers?" When the keepers returned, Toby was led back onto the truck and into his cage, and they all returned to the reserve.

On Tiny's next visit, Toby eagerly shared his experience. "We just looked at each other. I wanted to go out and be with them, to see where they lived and how they got their food, but they just walked away when they realized I was not free. Oh, Tiny, what can I do? I really wanted to go with them." Tiny sat very close to his friend and listened as a good friend would.

The keepers continued to take Toby out to meet the tigers. Each time the tigers stayed longer. They even began to play with him. Toby would put his paw up to the bars, and they would try to touch it with their paws. It became a game of Can You Catch My Paw. They really enjoyed being together.

All this time, Tiny was meeting new friends on his ventures around the reserve. He met a mouse family who lived in the keepers' cabin and another who lived in the canteen where they ate. He enjoyed visiting and playing with the family who lived in the canteen because the kitchen was there and there was always lots to eat. Tiny spent more and more time away from home and less and less time visiting Toby. But when they did see each other, they were still best friends.

One day, when Tiny was visiting his friends in the keepers' cabin, he overheard some keepers saying that soon two old tigers would be arriving. Tiny listened carefully because he knew Toby would  be interested to know about this. When Tiny told Toby about the old tigers, he listened but wasn't very interested. He was too busy thinking of the tigers he saw in the jungle and how he would like to be free with them.

One morning, as Toby was eagerly waiting to be taken to the jungle, he saw a big truck drive up and two tigers being led down the ramp. He remembered what Tiny had told him, and now he was curious to see the new tigers. He watched very carefully as the keepers led them past his cage on their way to a nearby cage that had been empty for some time.

Just at that moment, Tiny rushed in with more news. Tiny said, "Guess what? Remember Ralph? Well, he *did* get a job with a circus working with tigers. When the circus owners decided two of their tigers were too old to work, he told them about this

 reserve and that it would be a good place for them to retire. What do you think of that?"

The two friends just looked at each other.

"Are you thinking what I'm thinking?" they both said at once.

Tiny was more excited than ever. Now he had some real detective work to do. He said a quick good-bye to his friend and scurried off to the old tigers' cage to see what he could learn.

As he entered the cage, Tiny moved slowly so he would not be heard. He quickly hid behind some exercise toys that were scattered about the cage, and then he began to watch and listen. At first, the tigers walked around and around, trying to become familiar with their new home. After a while, when evening came, the tigers lay next to each other for warmth and comfort. They began remembering and talking of how they came to be in this place. The mama tiger said, "Do you remember how it was when we lived in the jungle with our little cub? We were so happy."

The daddy tiger answered, "Yes, but it all changed when we had to leave our little son hidden from the men who captured us. What a frightful night."

"All these years, I have missed our little boy so very much. Not a day goes by that I don't think of him. He was so young. Do you think he was able to find food? It must have been so scary and hard for him to grow up alone."

"It was difficult for all of us. We not only left our son and home, but we were taken to a strange place and taught things that were not natural for us. Remember how hard it was to learn to stand on a little drum? My feet kept slipping off."

The tigers laughed at this memory. "What about learning to jump through a big ring? That wasn't any fun. And when they set the ring on fire, I was so afraid my fur would burn!"

In a quiet voice, Papa said, "Look at us now, old and no longer wanted in the circus."

Mama tried to look on the bright side when she said, "But we did get used to performing, and it was fun to see the children and crowds enjoying our show. We are lucky to be retired and living in a place where we can grow old together."

Tiny had heard enough. In his mind, there was no doubt about it; he was sure these tigers were Toby's parents. Although it was late, he scurried back to Toby's cage to tell him what he had heard. Toby was asleep when Tiny woke him by shouting in his ear, *"I found your parents!"*

Toby raised his head so quickly that Tiny fell down with a big bump.

Toby said, "I'm sorry, Tiny, you really surprised me. Are you hurt? Tell me everything. I want to know all about my parents."

The story tumbled out of Tiny's mouth so fast that Toby could hardly keep up with what he was saying. He did hear that they missed him and his mom thought about him every day. Although he missed his parents, Toby was relieved and happy to know that they had been safe and brought joy to so many boys and girls. Toby asked Tiny, "How can we let them know I was rescued and am living in the same reserve? They will be so surprised! I can hardly wait."

Tiny yawned and said, "Let me sleep on it tonight. I'll be back in the morning so we can work on a plan."

As soon as Tiny woke the next morning, his brain began to think of a way to reunite Toby with his parents. They had to act fast because Toby was soon to be released into the jungle. Tiny rushed in to visit Toby, shouting, "*I got it, I got it!* What do you think of this? When they take you past your parents' cage on the way to the truck for your visit to the jungle, why don't you just sit down and play like you are sick? That way your parents can see you and you can let them know you are their son. You are too big to move, so the keepers will probably let you rest there for a little while."

That sounded good to Toby. When he was led out of his cage, he hung his head down and walked *very* slowly. When he was in front of his parents' cage, he stopped and lay down.

The keepers didn't know what to think. They let him lie while they discussed what to do. One of them went to ask the doctor what should be done. While he was gone, Toby looked at his parents, chuffed softly, and slightly wagged his tail. From their cage, they looked at him very carefully and sniffed.

"Could this be our son? He was such a little cub when we last saw him. It would be hard to recognize him now, but he seems to recognize us, and he does have a familiar scent."

When the keeper returned, he told his partner, "The doctor says that sometimes when an animal is not well, it helps to have him share a cage with other animals like himself. They have a way of making each other feel better. This is especially true for tigers. They are used to living in groups and need each other."

"I think he's right. Besides, it couldn't hurt. We're getting Toby used to being with other tigers by taking him to the jungle, so why don't we just put him in the cage with these two old tigers? He will probably perk up quickly."

Oh, joy! thought Toby. *At last I will be reunited with my parents.* Toby had a hard time trying to look sad and sick as the keepers led him to the door of his parents' cage.

As soon as the tigers were alone together, they sniffed each other, trying to find something familiar that would let them know they were family. *So far, so good,* thought Toby. When they had had enough sniffing, they settled down and began to visit. Toby knew these were his parents because Tiny told him so, but the old tigers weren't sure that Toby was their son because he had been just a cub the last time they saw him.

Toby spoke first. "When I was very young, my parents hid me in the jungle from men who were capturing tigers. My parents never returned, but I was found by keepers from this reserve and brought here to live. I have missed my mom and dad for so long."

The old tigers could hardly believe what they were hearing. Toby's story fit the memories they had of leaving their son alone in the jungle the night they were captured. At last, and after so many years, the family was reunited. The old tigers licked Toby all over to let him know they were his parents and that they too had missed him so very much. Then they told Toby about their life in the circus and how happy they were to be retired and to find their son. That night the family snuggled together and had the best dreams ever.

In the morning, before the keepers came to check on Toby, he told his mom and dad, "The keepers have been taking me to the jungle and leaving me so I could meet other tigers. I was always left in a cage, but we played and got to know each other. My friend, Tiny Mouse, sneaks around and listens to their plans. That's how I learned about you. They think I am old enough to go and live in the jungle with other tigers so I can have a real tiger's life. They also need to make room for the new animals they rescue."

When the keepers came to check on Toby, they saw that he had recovered and was quite content to be in the cage with the older tigers, so they returned to their cabin.

Tiny had been keeping an eye on Toby ever since he was put in the cage with his parents. After all, it was his idea for Toby to play sick. Tiny didn't want to interfere with this reunion, so he stayed out of sight and watched Toby and his parents get to know each other again. Now that Toby was in a cage with other tigers, Tiny was curious to know if the plans for Toby had changed. When the keepers left after seeing that Toby was not sick, Tiny followed them back to their cabin. He overheard them talking about their decision to leave Toby in the cage with the old tigers for a few more days.

They said, "If we leave Toby with the old tigers, we won't have to drive him to the jungle. It would be a lot easier than driving him back and forth every day. We can set him free the next time we take him out in the truck."

Hearing this, Tiny rushed to the tigers' cage to tell Toby what the keepers were planning. Toby was really glad to see Tiny. He wanted to introduce him to his parents and tell them what a good friend he was. Tiny was polite and happy to meet them, but he was also jittery and eager to share his news.

The tigers listened to every word. When Tiny finished, they looked at each other. This news was bittersweet. They were thrilled to know they would have a few more days together but very sad to know they would be separated again. Tiny didn't say anything, but he was especially sad knowing his best friend would soon be leaving.

Those last few days were the happiest days of their lives. Toby reunited with his parents, and Tiny shared in the happiness with his best friend. Every minute was spent talking about their adventures, remembering happy and sad times and just being together.

Sadly, one morning the keepers came and took Toby away. Mama and Papa Tiger could do nothing but watch as Toby was led to the truck that would take him to the jungle. They were very sad to lose their son again but happy, too, knowing he would be free to live with other tigers and to have his own family.

Tiny wanted to be with Toby for as long as he could, so when Toby was in his cage on the truck, he was surprised to see Tiny sitting beside him. The two best friends didn't say much. They just wanted to  be together. Each of them was thinking about the first time they met when Tiny was so hungry. They thought about the afternoons when Tiny's brothers and sisters would visit and they would all have so much fun together. A very special memory was Tiny's birthday, when they snuck out of the reserve and went exploring in the jungle. Finally, they recalled the surprise and joy when Toby's parents came to the reserve.

When the truck stopped and the keepers came to take Toby to be released into the jungle, the best friends, with tears in their eyes, snuggled for the last time and were thankful to have such a wonderful friendship.

ASK YOURSELF

1) Have you ever been *really, really* hungry? What did you do about it? Why was Tiny so hungry?

2) Do you know anyone who has been hungry? What does your community do to help the hungry people?

3) Have you ever done something you were told not to do? What happened? Did you get in trouble? What did Tiny do that he was told not to do? What did he do about it?

4) Has anybody ever made fun of you? What did you do about it? What happened to make it stop? Why did Tiny's brothers and sisters make fun of him?

5) Have your ever been made fun of at school? If so, what did you do about it?

6) What happened to Toby to make him feel sad?

7) Have you ever made fun of anyone? Why? What happened?

8) Have you ever seen anyone made fun of? Did you do anything about it? Why or why not?

9) Have you ever felt lonely or scared? What made you feel this way? What happened to make these feelings go away?

10) Why did Toby's parents hide him in the bushes? Do you think his parents did the right thing? How do you think he felt when he was found?

11) Have you ever found a lost animal? What did you do?

12) What do your parents do to protect you? Does this sometimes make you angry and restricted? Does it ever make you feel not loved?

13) Do you show thanks to your parents and family members for what they do to protect you?

14) Do you have a best friend who helps you and does special things for you?

15) Do you keep secrets with your friend? Is it hard to keep a secret?

16) What secret did Tiny and Toby have?

17) What did Tiny do for Toby that was so special and important? What did Toby do for Tiny that was so special?

18) Have you ever found something you had lost? How did it make you feel?

19) What did Toby find that was so special? How do you think he felt? How did Tiny feel about helping his friend find his parents? How do you think Toby's parents felt?

20) Have you ever had to say goodbye to a friend? Did you think you would ever meet him or her again? How do you think you would you feel if you could be with your friend again?

APPRECIATION

To Bob Singer for his guidance and encouragement

To Ethel Otchis for having confidence in me

To Nancy Willett for her valuable
literary suggestions

To Betsy Harris for her enthusiastic
support and editing skills

To Tony Seaman for his encouragement
and belief in me

To Ray Schmidler for his consultation,
creativity, and untiring support

ABOUT THE AUTHOR

Eva Schmidler is an educa-
tor with a love of animals.
Born in Texas, she has taught
American children in France
and Germany and in California.
She currently resides with her
husband in Georgia to be near
their two sons and granddaughter. This is her first
book. To learn more about the author and her book
visit: www.tinymakesafriendbook.com

ABOUT THE ILLUSTRATOR

Toby Mikle is a professional children's book illus-
trator and has illustrated over 200 books. His favorite part of the process is taking someone's dream
and making it a reality. Visit his website at: www.
mybookillustrator.com

Use the following pages to
DRAW PICTURES OF FRIENDS
THAT SHOW HOW YOU HELP EACH OTHER

Use the following pages to
DRAW PICTURES OF FRIENDS
THAT SHOW HOW YOU HELP EACH OTHER

Use the following pages to
DRAW PICTURES OF FRIENDS
THAT SHOW HOW YOU HELP EACH OTHER

Printed in the United States
By Bookmasters